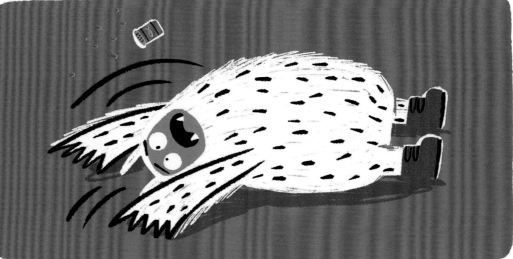

Not Yet, Yeti

Written by
Bethany V. Freitas

Illustrated by
Maddie Frost

CLARION BOOKS
AN IMPRINT OF HARPERCOLLINS PUBLISHERS • BOSTON • NEW YORK

For Teddy and Henry,
who teach me something
new every day —B.V.F.

For anyone (big or small) starting
something new. Never stop trying.
Never stop dreaming. —M.F.

This book was created in
consultation with Molly Picardi
and Shanna Schwartz of the
Teachers College Reading and
Writing Project.

Not Yet, Yeti
Copyright © 2022 by HarperCollins Publishers LLC

clarionbooks.com

The illustrations in this book were done in Photoshop with Kyle T. Webster digital brushes.
The text was set in Fontoon ITC Std.
Book design by Stephanie Hays

The Library of Congress Cataloging-in-Publication Data is available.

ISBN: 978-0-358-45025-2

Manufactured in Italy
10 9 8 7 6 5 4 3 2 1
4500844706

It's Yeti's first day of school. He has his backpack and his
lunch box. He has his red sneakers and a good-luck hug.
Yeti is excited. Yeti is ready.

School is full of friends he hasn't met yet.

And toys he hasn't played with yet.

And things he hasn't tried yet.

"Maybe not yet, Yeti.

"But I can see how hard you're working," his teacher says.

"Let's take a deep breath and try again."

Writing *is* hard for Yeti. He'll try again later.

Maybe.

At snack time, one student gets to feed the class fish.
And the teacher chooses . . .

CHOMP CHOMP

But Yeti is scared of fish!

Yeti CAN'T feed the fish!

"Not YET, Yeti!"
say his classmates.
"But you can try again."

"Great first day, everyone!"
the teacher says.

"And remember: We all get
to try again tomorrow."

Yeti's first day of school is over.

He just doesn't want to leave yet!

BETHANY V. FREITAS is a grownup who still reminds herself that just because she hasn't mastered something yet doesn't mean she never will. She lives in Massachusetts with her husband and two kids who are all passionate about trying new things.

MADDIE FROST has always wanted to be a picture book author and illustrator. Since she was very small, she wrote stories, drew every day, and never stopped trying to make her dreams come true. She believes anything is possible if you don't give up. She lives in Massachusetts with her husband and dogs. Learn more about Maddie and her books at maddie-frost.com.